P9-DOA-713

RADIO BOY

Story by SHARON PHILLIPS DENSLOW
Pictures by ALEC GILLMAN

SIMON & SCHUSTER BOOKS FOR YOUNG READERS

I would like to acknowledge the Pogue Library at Murray State University;
the Wrather West Kentucky Museum; and Robert H. Lochte, Ph.D.,
assistant professor, Department of Journalism/Radio-TV, and his associate, Larry Albert,
chief engineer at MST TV-11, for assistance generously offered
during my research for this book. —A. G.

SIMON & SCHUSTER BOOKS FOR YOUNG READERS
An imprint of Simon & Schuster Children's Publishing Division
1230 Avenue of the Americas
New York, NY 10022

Designed by Christy Hale
The text of the book is set in Caslon 76.
The illustrations were done in pen and ink and watercolor.
Manufactured in Hong Kong by South China Printing Company (1988) Ltd.
10 9 8 7 6 5 4 3 2 1

Library of Congress Cataloging-in-Publication Data
Denslow, Sharon Phillips.
Radio boy / story by Sharon Phillips Denslow ; pictures by Alec Gillman — 1st ed.
p. cm. Summary: In this fictionalized account of the childhood of Nathan Stubblefield,
who patented several inventions, the young boy fixes his neighbor's new telephone.
ISBN 0-689-80295-1
1. Stubblefield, Nathan Beverly, 1860–1928—Childhood and youth—Juvenile fiction.
[1. Stubblefield, Nathan Beverly, 1860–1928—Childhood and youth—Fiction. 2. Inventors—Fiction.]
I. Gillman, Alec, ill. II. Title.
PZ7.D433Rad 1995
[E]—dc20 93-36281
CIP AC

To Daddy, who, when I was little, showed me the old Stubblefield cabin site,
overgrown with weeds and marked only with a rusty pump handle...and
to Dr. L. J. Hortin, who wrote about Nathan B. Stubblefield
and worked to have him remembered in history...and
to my nephew, Eli Thomas Siress (1977-1992), who
liked knowing about things, too...and
to all the kids living in small places everywhere
who dream big
—S. P. D.

To Elizabeth & Cameron
—A. G.

There was a radio boy once in a small farmers' town in Kentucky.

The town had a square with a brick courthouse where farmers gathered and sat and visited and whittled and spit. There was a mill for grinding corn and a warehouse for the burley and dark-fired tobacco they pulled to town in heavy wagons.

There was a railroad track just north of town.

South of town there was a lumber mill to cut the wood the farmers cleared from the flat land and a sorghum mill, run by Mr. Gainey White, to grind the tall, stout sorghum canes into dark, sweet syrup.

To the west of town there was a pigeon roost where thousands and thousands of long-tailed pigeons rested each night.

And at the edge of town, under the pigeon flyway, was the house where the radio boy lived.

No one in Murray knew that Nathan B. was a radio boy, but they knew Nathan was always making contraptions out of coils and wires and barrels and crates.

When friends saw him with a strange package from St. Louis or Chicago, they'd ask, "What you inventing now, Nathan B.?"

"Electricals," Nathan would say with a determined nod.

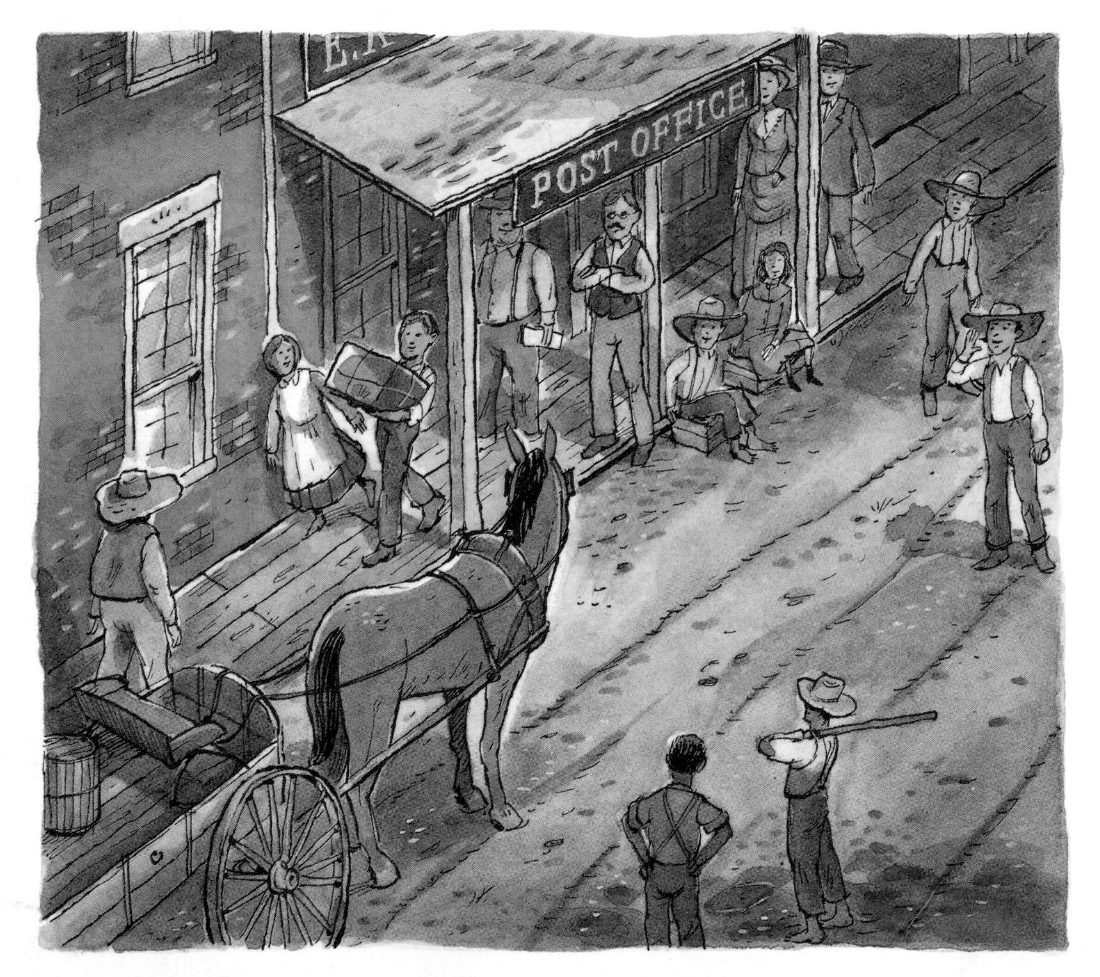

The town dogs always followed Nathan and his loaded-down wagon back from the post office. Talker would be out in front leading the way, the speckled Folsom brothers would be jumping around the wagon, and Gainey White's dog, Old Dutch, would be trailing stiff-legged behind.

None of the dogs except for Old Dutch, who was deaf, would venture past the front of Nathan's house, though. They'd stop and bark for fifteen minutes as Nathan pulled the wagon to the brooder house where he had his workshop; then they would turn silently back toward town. But Old Dutch would lie down in the dirt by the brooder house door, not hearing any of the crackling or sparking pops coming from inside.

People were very curious, especially Mr. Gainey White. What was Nathan fiddling with?

Sometimes when Nathan was between projects and Gainey's mill was closed for the day, they walked around Murray talking of things to come. Gainey was always interested in Nathan's talk about inventing.

Nodding at the gas lamps, Nathan told his friend, "Someday there'll be lights burning with electricity in towns everywhere."

Mr. Gainey White shook his head and murmured, "Electric lights in Murray. What next?"

Nathan whispered softly, "Everything."

One evening, coming back from visiting his brother Tom's farm, Mr. Gainey turned down the road past Nathan's. The front window of the brooder house was propped open, and inside he could see a glass jar burning brighter than the big lamps on the square.

Mr. Gainey stopped his buggy.

"That one of those electricity lights?" he called.

"Sort of," Nathan said as the light died out. He grinned. "But I've got something better than that to show you, Mr. Gainey."

Nathan handed Mr. Gainey a cone made of wood and metal, attached to a long wire. "Put this up to your ear and listen," he said.

Carefully letting the wire out behind him, Nathan walked to the sweet gum tree near Mr. Gainey's wagon. The horse turned its head to watch Nathan talk into another cone attached to the other end of the wire.

"Can you
hear me,
Mr. Gainey?"

Mr. Gainey hollered, "I can hear you loud as day, Nathan!"

Nathan motioned for Gainey to talk through the receiver.

Mr. Gainey put the cone to his mouth.

"Someday
you're
going
to be
famous,
Nathan B."

Nathan's workshop outgrew the brooder house. His machines and experiments filled the back porch and an empty stable and a room in the attic.

When Mr. Gainey's cousin in St. Louis wrote a few years later to say he had a new telephone but that it crackled in his ear so he could hardly hear and no one was able to fix it, Mr. Gainey wrote back and told him to send it to his young friend Nathan.

Gainey's cousin laughed at the idea of somebody in a farm town working on his new telephone. Why, no one in Murray even owned a telephone! He changed his mind, though, the day after a heavy storm turned his telephone into an impossible crackling box. He disconnected it himself and sent it by train to Murray.

Nathan B. worked on that telephone for a week. When word got around that Nathan was working on a real St. Louis telephone, a crowd often gathered at Nathan's porch.

He had to stop several times a day to let folks try it out.

With its new receiver, the telephone was shipped back to Mr. Gainey's cousin in St. Louis. His telegram came the next week: "Tell Nathan Stubblefield I've got the best telephone in town!"

Mr. Gainey invited Nathan to celebrate his success with molasses cake and lemonade. The whole town of Murray turned out.

"What else can you do, Nathan?" Gainey asked from the darkening porch.

Most of the guests had already gone home, walking or riding their wagons through the Kentucky twilight.

Overhead thousands of pigeons flew home in deep, ruffling waves of feathers toward their roost.

"I can make telephones without wires," Nathan answered.

Gainey White stared at Nathan. "Nobody can do that," he said.

Nathan smiled. "Not yet."

With the leftover tin of molasses cake under his arm, the radio boy walked home thinking about voices moving through the air as easily as the sounds of the passenger pigeons' soft, fluttering wings.

AUTHOR'S NOTE

Nathan Beverly Stubblefield (1860-1928) was a real boy inventor from Murray, Kentucky. Nathan patented several inventions as a young man, including a vibrating telephone (of which one of his neighbors in 1887 said, "It was the best I have ever talked through"), electrical batteries, and a wireless telephone. The word *radio* was not generally used at the time of Nathan's demonstrations of his wireless telphone, but his invention that transmitted voices through the air without wires was what we now call a radio. As early as 1885, Nathan could broadcast without wires. His most famous broadcast was held on the Potomac River on March 20, 1902. The *Washington Post* described the first ship-to-shore broadcast as having sounds "so distinct as to startle the hearers at the receiver."

The characters and the sequence of events in this story are fictional—with the exception, of course, of that remarkable radio boy from Murray, Kentucky, Nathan B. Stubblefield.

Nathan Stubblefield and his induction telephone circa 1902